The Christmas Fairy

To the lovely Haynes family: Emma, Stuart,
Amy, Charlie, Saffron, and Theo; and
in loving memory of Hattie
A. B.

To Elsa, Ella, and Maria
Love from Rosi B x

Text copyright © 2016 by Anne Booth
Illustrations copyright © 2016 by Rosalind Beardshaw

Nosy Crow and its logos are trademarks of Nosy Crow Ltd.
Used under license.

First U.S. edition 2017

Library of Congress Catalog Card Number pending
ISBN 978-0-7636-9629-0

17 18 19 20 21 22 FGF 10 9 8 7 6 5 4 3 2 1

Printed in Shenzhen, Guangdong, China

This book was typeset in Baskerville Old Face.
The illustrations were done in mixed media.

Nosy Crow
an imprint of
Candlewick Press
99 Dover Street
Somerville, Massachusetts 02144

www.nosycrow.com
www.candlewick.com

The Christmas Fairy

Anne Booth

illustrated by

Rosalind Beardshaw

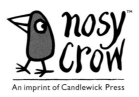

nosy crow

An imprint of Candlewick Press

Clara was a chatterbox,
a fairy full of fun.
She loved to sing and dance
and bring a smile to everyone.

And every day at fairy school
she wished that she could be
a proper Christmas fairy
on a sparkly Christmas tree.

So Clara was excited
when she heard Miss Petal call,
"It's **Christmas fairy** lesson time.
I'm going to teach you all!

You'll learn to stand like statues while you hold a **fairy** pose
and stay as **quiet** as a mouse while standing on your toes.
And then you must be **sensible**—don't wave your wands around.
Now, Clara, listen **carefully**,
and **please** don't make a sound."

"We'll practice hard all month,

and then you'll show me what you know.

And afterward I'll take you to

a **special** Christmas show.

You'll hear a bluebird singer chirp a song you **won't** forget,

and then a **graceful** dancing swan will leap and pirouette.

Next some funny penguin clowns will jump up and be clever—
I'm sure the Christmas Show this year will be the best one ever!"

"But first," Miss Petal said,
"let's practice standing in a pose.
Remember to stay very still,
and do not scratch your nose."

So Clara balanced on one leg,
but gave a little **giggle** . . .

which turned into a **wobble** and
became a **great big wriggle!**

"Now, fairies," said Miss Petal,
"stay as quiet as can be.
And think how **happy** you will feel
when you are on a tree."

So Clara tried her **very** best, but somehow it went wrong.

Her quiet happy thoughts became a **hum** and then a **song**!

"Be sensible," Miss Petal said, "and line up two by two."

"Oh, let's be monkeys!" Clara laughed.

The others giggled, too.

"Look!" Clara said and reached up high. "Now I'm a tall giraffe!"

"Now, come on, girls!" Miss Petal said.

"This is no time to laugh."

Then just before the Christmas Show,
Miss Petal gave a test.
"Let's all be Christmas fairies now.
Please try your very best.

"Now, hold your fairy poses, please. Be silent and no wiggles."
So Clara tried . . . but got an itchy arm and then the giggles!

Miss Petal sighed. "That's not at all
what Christmas fairies do.
You always sing, or dance, or laugh.
What **shall** I do with you?"

And when the fairies formed a line
and set off for the show,
poor Clara dawdled at the back,
her footsteps very slow.

"I'll **never** be a proper fairy on a Christmas tree.

I'm a noisy, wriggly giggler, and I **wish** I wasn't me."

But then she heard a jingling sound,
looked up, and saw a sleigh.
"Ho, ho, there, Clara," Santa cried.
"I'm landing now, make way!"

"We **need** you, Clara," Santa said.
"That's why I've come along.
The Christmas Show's in trouble.
Almost **everything's**
gone wrong."

"The little bluebird's lost his voice
and **cannot** make a sound.
The ballerina **bumped**
her head while twirling
round and round.

The penguin clowns **slipped** on the ice, and now they're quite a sight.

If no one takes their places, there will be no show **tonight!**"

"We need a special fairy who is full of **life** and **fun,**
who dances, sings, and laughs and jokes,
and cheers up **everyone.**
You're **such** a happy fairy—
it's simply who you are.
You make us smile, no matter what.
So would you be our star?"

"Who, me?" said little Clara.

"Can I really play each part?"

"Of course you can," said Santa,

"and the show's about to start!"

So Clara stepped onto the stage
and sang a Christmas song.
And **everybody** watching clapped
their hands and sang along.

Next Clara stretched her arms out wide
and twirled across the floor.
The audience all gasped and cheered
and loudly cried for more!

Then Clara made the fairies laugh
(and all the others, too)
by trumpeting and roaring
like the creatures in a zoo.

When Clara finished, everyone stood up and gave three cheers.
And Santa boomed, "Your Christmas show's
the **best** I've seen for years!

Some Christmas fairies make us sing
and laugh, and so you see,
not **every** Christmas fairy
has to stand still on a tree.

Oh, well done, Clara!" Santa said.
"You **really** saved the show.
And now a gift for everyone—
it's out here in the snow."

He led them to a Christmas tree,

so beautiful and green.

"Oh, thank you," whispered Clara.

"It's the best I've ever seen."

Then all the fairies climbed
into the branches of the tree,
with Clara on the very top,
as **happy** as could be.